Shattered Glass

A Brains Benton Adventure

By
Charles E. Morgan, III

Based on characters created by
Charles Spain Verral. (1904-1990)

Illustrated by
Shannon Stirnweis

To Charles and Randy

Copyright © 2012 by Charles E. Morgan, III

ALL RIGHTS RESERVED

Shattered Glass

Contents

Chapter	Page
I. Up on the Roof	7
II. The Shattered Glass	13
III. The Lab	21
IV. The Search	29
V. The Vandal	35

Up on the Roof

Chapter 1

I'll never forget that night, even if I live to be a hundred! It was the night that changed everything. It was the night that I became a private investigator!

First, I guess I'd better explain.

My full name is James McDonald Carson, but my family and friends call me Jimmy. I live at 43 Maple Street in the town of Crestwood. I attend Taylor Elementary School.

My family is your normal run of the mill type. My dad is an accountant at the gas company. He works close enough that he can sometimes come home for lunch. My mom runs the household and is a member of a bunch of different clubs. She's even the head of one! I have a sister, Ann. She's older than I am and never lets me forget it.

Crestwood is a swell place. It's small, but still has plenty to do. To the south of town we have the Indian River. About twenty miles to the north there's Lake Carmine. And in between we have hills and mountains. We get four seasons, a real spring, summer, winter, and fall. People say it's beautiful around here. I guess they're right.

The town has a radio station, a movie theatre, and a park. We have a drugstore where you can get the best ice-cream sundae around! We even have a semi-pro baseball team called the Crestwood Colts. The town might be small, but it has just about everything you could want. And if for some reason if you ever got bored, Crestwood College always has something cool going on.

Like most towns, businesses are closed on Sundays, and the streets roll up about 5 o'clock weekdays. It's the last place in the world that you would think a crime would happen. But sometimes it does. And on that Friday, near the end of the school year, I was just about to witness one firsthand.

It was evening and I was coming back from Randy Steven's house. I had gone over to get paid. You see, Randy has a newspaper route delivering the *Crestwood Daily Ledger* and I'm his substitute. He uses me when he can't make deliveries or just wants a day off. He's an older kid, about a year older than Ann.

Having a paper route was a big deal around here and I was hoping that when Gary went off to college, I might be able to get his route.

Darkness had settled in across the town and the street lights had blinked on. I was riding south on Washington Avenue when out of the blue a thought sprang into my mind. I made a right on Spruce Street and pedaled towards my elementary school.

Over the previous two Friday nights, Taylor Elementary had been vandalized. Someone had thrown a rock through one of the classroom windows.

On a whim I decided to check it out.

I turned into the school's parking lot and stopped and listened. All I heard was the chirping of crickets.

Maybe I had been watching too many private detective shows on TV, but I decided I wanted to stakeout the school. I didn't need to be home for a bit, so I had time to put the place under surveillance.

At first I thought of hiding out in the wooded median strip that separated the school from the Spruce Street. It was about ten yards thick and ran the entire length of the front of Taylor Elementary. An entrance way onto the school property and an exit back to the street bookend the far sides of the raised strip of grass and trees. A road ran between them directly in front of the school. It was used to drop students off.

But the more I thought about it, I realized that area would be the most likely place the vandal or vandals would hide when they threw the rock.

So I decided to do something bold.

I looked over at the side of the two story brick school. I smiled as I spotted the ladder that ran up the building.

Jeepers! I had always wanted to climb that ladder, even back in first grade.

I ditched my bike in a path that cut through the woods on the side of school property. Before I walked out into the open, I stood there in the shadows and scanned the area like a British ship looking for a U-boat.

The coast was clear.

I scurried like a bunny across the parking lot to the side of the school.

My heart was pounding in my throat and butterflies took off in my stomach.

I had never done anything like this before!

I grabbed a cool metal rung on the ladder started to climb.

I didn't take my time either. I shot up that ladder like the mercury in a hot thermometer.

I knew I was trespassing and I didn't want to get caught!

When I stepped over the edge onto the roof it was like stepping into a different world. A cool gentle breeze blew on my now sweaty face. The roof top was tarred gravel. Everything was flat.

I hunched over and crept toward the front of the school. As I got closer to the edge, I got all the way down and started to crawl.

I took up a position laying flat on the roof.

The view was amazing!

I liked looking down on everything. And I could see a little way into the woods that separated the school from Spruce Street.

I spied the white metal flagpole with the gold ball on top. I smiled as I remembered the time when I'd come up to the school one evening with a bunch of guys a couple of years earlier. The flag was down for the day and I had swung on the cord like Tarzan through the trees.

It had been real neat and a lot of fun. I wasn't heavy enough back then to do any damage. We all took turns---

"What are you doing here?"

At the sound of the words interrupting the silence my heart nearly stopped and I had the sinking feeling of being caught. The voice came from behind me and if I'd been standing there I might have accidently jumped off the roof because of fright!

Wide eyed I turned and looked. A figure was standing behind me. I couldn't tell who it was because of the shadows. But I could tell it was kid.

I crawled away from the edge because I didn't trust him or my frazzled nerves. When I felt safe I finally stood up.

I squinted through the darkness and finally recognized him.

He was a kid who was in 6th grade like I was, but he was in another class. I had Mrs. Winter for my teacher and he had Mr. Thomas.

Over the years we had indeed had some of the same teachers. I think it was first, second, and third grade.

I didn't really know him and I don't even know if we had ever talked before. He was sort of an odd duck. He always had his nose stuck in a book.

All the kids called him Brains. He had earned nickname because he was so smart. He came by his gray matter naturally though as both his parents taught at Crestwood College. He could have been called Stretch, because he was so tall, or Bones, because he was so skinny, or Red, because of the color of his hair. He could have even been nicknamed Specs, because he wore glasses. But no, the kids had hung the moniker *Brains* on him, and it had stuck like glue.

"You're Brains--- err, Barclay Benton," I said.

"You can call me Brains. I'm not particularly fond of Barclay. It makes me sound like I should be a butler."

He smiled and I laughed. Odd duck or not, I liked him right away.

"You're Jimmy Carson."

"Right," I said.

"What are you doing up here?" he asked again.

"I was watching to see if the vandal showed up."

"How do I know you aren't the vandal?" Brains asked.

"Do I look like a vandal?" I snapped.

"I don't know what a vandal looks like."

He had a point. We stared at each other for a moment.

"Hey, where'd you come from anyway?" I asked.

"I was watching you. When you started up the ladder I went for cover over there."

Brains jerked his thumb.

I followed the direction and saw a large brick chimney. It was probably six foot square and six feet tall.

"I believe that's where the furnace is vented," Brains said.

He looked at me. "I know you aren't the vandal, Jimmy."

"How do you know?" I asked.

"I observed you. It was apparent that you were trying to ascertain where to conduct your surveillance. Besides, there's nothing to vandalize up here. And of course with a prowl car parked out there on Spruce Street the real vandal should be deterred."

"The cops are here?" I exclaimed. I almost shouted it, but was smart enough to keep my voice down.

What type of private eye was I anyway? I had totally missed it!

"Maybe we should get down before we get caught!"I whispered.

"We're already up here. We might as well stay."

"Wait a minute. Why are you up here?" I asked.

"For the same reason you are. I want to catch the perpetrator."

Man! That kid sure did talk fancy! He was the type of guy who would read a dictionary for fun.

"But do you really think the cops will scare the vandal away?" I asked.

"Certainly. They will be a deterrent as long as they are out front. However once they vacate---"

Suddenly, the quite of the night was shattered by the sound broken glass!

The Broken Window

Chapter 2

After the initial shock, Brains and I hurried over to the edge of the roof at the front of the school. I heard him mutter something about being distracted. He sounded disgusted. But he was talking to himself, not to me.

When we got edge, we looked down. We couldn't see anything unusual. All was quiet and still.

"What should we do?" I hissed.

"Let's go investigate!" Brains answered excitedly.

He took off for the ladder with long loping strides. I was right behind him.

Once on the ground, Brains took off running. He had a big lead on me but I started to catch up to him when we rounded the corner to the front of the building. I was right behind him as we crossed the pavement of the main entranceway of the school.

I had run so fast my baseball cap had almost flown off my head the way Willie Mays' does when he's tracking a ball in centerfield. But at the last instant I reached up and pulled my hat back down.

Brains came to a stop in front of the outside where the classrooms started.

"I think it was somewhere around here that the perpetrator broke the window," he said.

"Yeah," I agreed.

We looked at the windows. It was hard to see which one was broken because it was so dark. I tried viewing at an angle to see if I could catch glare in the glass.

"There!" I said pointing.

We hustled over to the window and looked. There was a hole in the center of the window about the size of a basketball. The jagged glass looked like teeth.

Suddenly a booming voice came from behind us.

"I knew it was juvenile delinquents!"

For the second time that night I heard a voice from behind me. I was so shocked I almost keeled over dead on the spot!

I turned around and there standing on the sidewalk behind Brains and me were two policemen. They held the beam from their flashlights in our face. I gulped. I had recognized the one who had spoken right away. It was the number one cop of the Crestwood Police Department. It was none other than Chief Hadley himself!

I wanted crawl in a hole and hide.

The chief took himself and his job very seriously. As serious as a heart attack! Chief Hadley liked to dress the part too. As usual he was in his full dress uniform. And brother let me tell you he had enough brass to equip a band!

"Who are you?" he barked as if he were a Marine drill sergeant. "What're your names?"

I opened my mouth and tried to speak. But I was so honest to goodness scared that nothing came out. I just stood there with my jaw going up and down like a ventriloquist dummy without a ventriloquist.

I didn't know what to do. I realized that Chief Hadley thought we had broken the window and he believed he'd caught us red-handed! I had never been in trouble before in my life. Well at least not like this.

If Brains was scared however, he never showed it.

"Good evening, Chief Hadley," Brains said in a voice as smooth as glass. "My name is Barclay Benton and this is Jimmy Carson. We are not *juvenile delinquents*, as you so eloquently put it. But rather concerned citizens."

I don't know what I was expecting but it wasn't this. I just stared at Brains. So did Chief Hadley and the other police officer.

Suddenly I got brave.

"Yeah, we were---"

Brains stepped on my foot.

"Oww!" I howled as I hopped up and down doing a one footed war dance.

"Oh, sorry, Jimmy," Brains said. Then he ignored me and continued. "Chief Hadley, if you will please shine your light over here, I would like to show you something. I believe I can prove to you we did not vandalize the school."

Suddenly my foot didn't hurt anymore. I wanted to see this too.

Chief Hadley stepped up and shined his light on the window.

"So?" he said losing patience.

"You don't see it?" Brains asked.

I knew I sure didn't. It was just saw a hole.

"What!" Hadley demanded. He stepped forward and shined the light inside the classroom. "I see the rock in there that you threw through the window."

He turned and smiled.

I didn't know what game Brains was playing but I knew he better stop it before we got thrown into the clink and Hadley threw away the key!

"Please note the glass on the ground," Brains said with a sweeping hand as if presenting royalty.

"You're a genius, Benton" Hadley snapped. "With a broken window you get glass on the ground."

"Chief. This window was broken from the inside. Almost all of the glass is right here on the ground…outside! And we don't have keys to get inside."

The other officer spoke up. "He's right, Chief. A thrown rock would have take most of the glass inside."

Hadley just stood there and made a *harrumph* sound. I could tell he still wanted to nail us for the broken window.

"And to further facilitate our innocence," Brains said, "please note that there is a little bit of matter here on this jagged edge. I believe it is skin. The perpetrator cut himself. And as you can see, Jimmy and I do not have as much as a scratch on our hands."

With that Brains held his hands up as if he was scrubbed for surgery. I did too. But behind my cut free hands, I wore a big relived smile on my face.

The two officers checked our hands.

"They're clean, Chief. I guess the vandal got away."

Hadley just glared at us. Then he said, "Don't let me ever catch you two hanging around here again!"

"Yes, sir!" we echoed.

With that, he then turned and marched off.

"Hey, Benton," the other policeman said. "That was pretty slick observation. Maybe you should consider being a cop someday."

"Thank you, Officer ah---"

"McKeon. I'm Officer McKeon. It was nice to meet you boys."

Off in the distance we heard Chief Hadley yell, "McKeon!"

"Coming, Chief!"

He tipped his cap and ran off.

Brains and I stood there for a second watching. When Officer McKeon was out of sight I turned to Brains.

"Golly!" I gushed. "That *was* great observations! I thought for sure we were going to get measured for striped suits!"

"It was nothing. It was obvious."

"Not to me," I said.

"It's because you look but do not see."

Huh?

We started to walk toward my bike.

"Hey, Brains. Why did you step on my foot?"

"I believe you were about to tell Chief Hadley that we were on the roof at the time of the vandalism."

"Yeah, so?"

As soon as I said it I knew.

Brains said, "He could have gotten us for *trespassing*."

We said the last word in unison.

"Chief Hadley wants a collar. It doesn't matter who. And any old charge will do," Brains stated.

"Creeps! You're right!"

I grabbed my bike. It turned out that Brains had parked his bike in the woods too. Only he didn't just stick his on the path. He had hidden it behind some bushes.

We got on our bikes and headed home.

As we rode along Spruce Street we talked.

"So, Jimmy, why did you stakeout the school tonight?"

"Well, I guess it was a spur of the moment thing. I just wanted to catch the guy."

"Do you like solving mysteries?"

I laughed out loud. I couldn't help it.

"Brains, I've never solved a mystery. But yeah, I'd like to. I've always wanted to be a private detective like Mike Hammer or even a secret agent like James Bond."

"I tend to fancy Sherlock Holmes myself," Brains said.

We had turned down Washington Avenue. Brains slowed down and then came to a stop at the intersection of Tinker Drive.

"I've got to go this way," he said.

"Okay," I said. "I guess I'll see ya around."

I started to pedal for home.

"Jimmy," Brains called out.

"Yeah?" I said slowing down.

"You want to start a private detective business with me?"

I turned the bike around and stopped. The street light lit the two of us up like actors on a stage.

"You serious?" I asked.

Kids as private detectives! I'd never heard of such a thing, - at least not in real life!

"Certainly I'm serious," Brains answered. "We both have an interest in criminology. And truth be told, I have been thinking seriously about this for a while. I have even been making preparations."

Preparations? I wanted to ask him what he meant by that, but I had to get home. It was getting late and I knew my folks would be getting worried.

"I need to get home," I said, "but maybe we can get together tomorrow to discuss it more."

"So you want to do it? You want to be partners?"

"Absolutely!"

"Very well, Jimmy. I have to go to the college with my father tomorrow morning. But I will stop by your house before I go with instructions for our meeting. Can you come over to my house around noon?"

"Sure," I said. "That will give me enough time to get my chores done."

"Excellent! What's your address?"

I gave it to him. Then we said goodnight.

As we biked our separate ways, little did I know that I had just met a person who would turn out to be my best friend. Not just during my school years, but for the rest of my life!

The Lab

Chapter 3

I lay in bed the next morning trying to talk myself into getting up.

I wasn't listening.

I heard the doorbell ring and someone open the front door. I then drifted off to sleep and dozed some more.

By the time I came down for breakfast, the aroma of bacon and coffee perfumed the air.

"Morning, Jimmy," my mom said. "How'd you sleep, dear?"

She was already dressed for the day. She wore a dress with pearls and heels. A print apron with different type of fruits on it was tied around her waist.

"Good," I replied.

I was quite the conversationalist in the morning!

"A boy dropped this envelope off for you this morning."

She handed me a white mailing envelope. It was sealed so I ripped it open.

I looked at it, blinked a couple of times, and tried to read it again.

"Who is it from?" she asked.

"A kid called Brains, Brains Benton," I replied.

"Is he the one whose parents teach at the college?"

"Yep," I said. "He and I are going to start hanging out together."

"That's great!" she said.

You see, my best friend, Charlie Poe, had moved away last summer and I hadn't really found someone else to play with. I'm sure my mom was excited about the prospect of me getting out of the house a bit more.

She put breakfast down in front of me and I dug in. I was famished! I read and reread the note as I ate.

It read:

```
Go down the alleyway between Chestnut Drive
and Channing Street. The third house on the right
is 56 Chestnut.
    Hide your bike in the bushes and the face
the north side of the garage.
    Press the third nail in the fourth board
from the bottom.
    Once you have memorized your instructions,
destroy this note
    See you at noon.
    Operative X
```

"For Pete's sake!" I said out loud.

"What is it, dear?"

"Aw, nothing, mom"

"Well how was it?"

"What?"

Your breakfast. French toast and bacon? Your favorite."

Holy cow! I had been so distracted reading that I hadn't even notice I had devoured one of my favorite all-time meals!

"Oh! It was great mom! Thanks!"

She was looking at me suspiciously while I chugged my glass of ice cold milk, cleared my dishes, and then gave her a kiss on the cheek.

She smiled.

Moms are great! It takes so little to make them happy.

"I'm gonna go do my chores." I said as I left the room.

Two hours later, after I'd mowed the yard and edged the sidewalk, I found myself turning down the alleyway that ran behind Benton's' house.

I counted off the houses and stopped at the third house.

I looked around as I crammed my bike between some hedges. No one saw me.

I hadn't been a boy scout, but I could certainly figure out which way was north by the sun.

I walked around to the front of the garage and faced north. It was a big old structure. Like most the garages in this part of town I knew it had been a coach house in the old horse-and-buggy days.

What confused me however was that the garage doors were standing open and Brains was nowhere in sight.

I stood there stumped.

I decided to do what the note said. I walked to the corner and kneeled down. I counted up four boards and pushed the third nail.

Nothing happened. I pushed again, harder.

"May I help you young man!"

I nearly jumped out of my skin! For the third time in less than twenty four hours someone had sneaked up on me.

Creeps! I'd better start paying better attention to what's behind me or else I'd wind up in the loony bin with shattered nerves!

I turned my head and stood up.

I found myself staring at a hatchet faced, little woman with cat eyed glasses. Her shrill voice matched her sharp face.

"Well!"

"Umm, I looking for, Brains," I said.

"There is no *Brains* living at this residence!"

She said the name as if it tasted sour on her tongue.

"Oh, sorry. I thought this was the Benton residence."

"It is! If you are looking for Barclay, he is not in that little corner you were playing with. He's upstairs in that *place* of his!"

She clucked her tongue in disgust, turned, and walked away.

When she was gone, I turned back around and faced north again. I held my hands out in despair. It made no sense!

I pulled the note out from my jean's pocket. I was sure glad that I hadn't thrown it away yet.

I reread it for probably the hundredth time. That's when I finally got it. The note said to face the north side of the building, not face north!

Man! Maybe my teachers were right. I'd better learn how to follow instructions better!

I jammed the piece of paper into my pocket and ran around to the back of the building.

I had to push my way through some bushes, but I finally was facing the north side of the garage!

I hit the third button on the fourth board. I knew if it didn't work I would try the other corner, but suddenly a metallic voice spoke.

"State your name and business."

"Umm, Jimmy Carson and ah, none of *your* business."

I laughed. I thought that was pretty clever, especially under the circumstances.

There was silence. Maybe Brains didn't think I was so funny.

Suddenly, a section of the garage slid open. Inside it was dark.

I took one last look at the sunlight. Hoped I'd see it again. Then I ducked down and stepped inside.

The panel immediately slid shut.

Creeps!

I stood there in inky black and I got to tell you I didn't like it. Not one bit!

A bluish light flickered on and I could make out a staircase in front of me.

Well that lady had said Brains was upstairs. So I started up.

As I climbed from the first step to the second I heard a click behind me.

Oh no, not again!

I turned to make sure no one was behind me.

Nope! Coast was clear.

I took another step.

Click!

I stopped again. That's when I realized the sound was coming behind and under me.

I took my toe and tapped the step behind me.

The staircase must have been spring loaded because the step had disappeared after I'd stepped off it!

Holy cow! What had I gotten myself into?

I skedaddled up the steps afraid that instead they might be on a timer. I certainly didn't want to risk sliding down the newly forming slope!

At the top of the stairs another panel slid open.

I stepped through and into another room. And brother let me tell you, what a room!

The place was a combination of science laboratory, a space ship, and a machine shop!

There were beakers, test tubes, gizmos and gadgets all over the place. I saw power tools as well as microscopes and a telescope.

Wow! The place had everything!

I looked at one table and there was what looked like a printing press on it with tools and parts surrounding it.

"Brains?" I called out.

Nothing. I was alone.

I checked my Timex watch. It was 12:05.

"Hmm" I muttered. "He must be late."

Suddenly a mirror on the far wall opened and out stepped Brains Benton dressed in a white lab jacket.

"No Jimmy, actually you are the one who's late. However I had calculated that the first time you came to our headquarters it would take you a bit to figure it out."

I wasn't sure if that was a dig at me or not. I just let it go.

"Brains, this place is amazing!"

"Thank you. You are the first person to ever see the lab."

"Not even your parents have seen it?"

"No adults are allowed."

Suddenly it all made sense.

"Yeah, that lady I met outside didn't seem too pleased about you being in here."

Brains smiled. "Ah, so you have met our petite little flower of a housekeeper, Mrs. Ray. She doesn't tend to agree with how my parents have reared me. She feels rather strongly that I have been given too much freedom."

"You're parents are A-Okay in my book!" I said enthusiastically.

Brains and I spent the next few hours discussing things. You know, this and that.

Anyway, he gave me a tour of the lab, or the headquarters of the newly founded, Benton and Carson International Detective Agency.

Brains had come up with the name and I gotta say I liked it a lot!

He told me he thought that I would be an ideal private eye. He'd said I would blend in better than he would if we were shadowing someone. You see, I was the average height and weight for a kid my age. I had brown hair and eyes. I also have some freckles that I hated, but my mom says are cute. The bottom line was, I would blend in real well in a crowd.

I'd never thought that being average would be a good thing. But in this circumstance I could see how it was.

He asked if it was okay with me he would be the president of the firm and that I could be the secretary-treasurer.

I told him that was just *peachy* with me!

"Hey, Brains, why did you sign the note Operative X?"

"It is a matter of security. I believe we should use code names when we are working on a case. That way our identities are protected if some dastardly criminal should happen to overhear us communicating."

"That makes sense," I said. "I guess I should be Operative Two."

"No, I was thinking Operative Three. Then no one will know how many operatives we really have."

"Hey, yeah! I like that."

Besides, the number three used to be the number that Babe Ruth had worn. If it was good enough for him it was certainly good enough for me!

"Very well, you shall be, Operative Three," Brains pronounced.

It sounded real good when Brains said it.

"So, Operative X, what are we going to do about the school vandal?"

"Well, Operative Three, that case has pretty much solved itself."

"How do you mean?"

"First off, the glass was broken from the inside. What's that mean? It's an inside job. Secondly, the little bit of matter that was on the jagged edge of glass means that whoever broke the window cut themselves."

Brains picked up a beaker.

"Let's say this is the rock," he said, "The person holds it and just plans to tap a hole through the glass. But the glass breaks easier than expected. His hand goes partially through the window. He pulls it back and, presto! He cuts the top of his hand."

"Why didn't he cut himself on the other windows?"

"Because before the latest incident he threw the rock from the outside---"

"And because the cops were there, he had to do it from inside, trying to make it look like the rock had also been thrown from outside!"

"Precisely, Operative Three!"

Brains said it so excitedly, I felt like I had just won a medal!

I think I could get use to this private detective biz!

"So whoever did it is an employee of the school," I continued.

Brains nodded. "So when we go to school on Monday, all we have to do is find someone with a band aid, bandaged, or cut hand."

"Yippee!" I cheered. We got them!"

The Search

Chapter 4

I was so excited that I felt something I'd never felt before. I actually couldn't wait to go to school!

But the next day was Sunday. My family and I went to church. I spied Brains up in the balcony and asked if I could go sit with him.

My folks said sure.

When I got up there, Brains reached into his suit jacket and pulled something out.

"What do you think?" he asked.

I looked at it. It was a card and it read:

**THE BENTON AND CARSON
INTERNATIONAL DETECTIVE AGENCY**

CONFIDENTIAL INVESTIGATIORS AND CRIMINOLOGISTS
MODERN SCIENTIFIC METHODS AND DEVICES USED

SHADOWING   FREE CONSULTATION
TRACING MISSING PERSONS   24-HOUR SERVICE

President: *Secretary-Treasurer:*

Barclay "Brains" Benton   James "Jimmy" Carson

"Holy smokes!" I whispered. "This is keen!"

Brains smiled. "After you went home last night, I finished fixing that old printing press. I produced this prototype early this morning. If you approve, this will be our business card."

Are you kidding me? This is great!"

"Keep it then," Brains said. "The type in the machine is already set."

"I can keep it? Golly! Thanks!"

As I stuck the card inside my suit pocket, I felt like a million bucks!

Well one thing I'd learned. When Brains did something, he did it first class!

I would have loved to spend the rest of the day after church hanging out with Brains in the lab. But my folks had other ideas. I had to go visit my aunt and her family. They live about an hour away. And by the time we got home that evening, it was time to "settle down," as my folks liked to say, and get ready for school the next day.

So I wound up not getting to see Brains again until Monday morning. We had made plans for where and when to meet as we'd walked out of church.

It was a good thing that my Safety Patrol post for the week was in front of the school. Otherwise I would have been stationed on some street corner and wouldn't have been able to meet up with Brains early in the morning. My job was to make sure that the kids, especially the younger ones, didn't run.

I know it's not exactly a glamorous job. But someone's got to do it!

I met Brains at my post in front of the school.

"Morning, Operative Three," Brains greeted happily.

"Morning, X! So what's the plan?"

I had about fifteen minutes until I had to be on duty.

"Let's walk around and see who's here. Pay special attention to the hands, especially the right one."

"Check" I said as we walked through the front doors.

"Let's go to the office first," Brains suggested.

We opened the door to the main office. It was where the only air-conditioned rooms in the whole school were located.

I guess that was an upside to being sent to the principal's office, not that I ever had been.

"Good morning, Barclay, James, how may I help you?"

It was Miss Brooks, the school's main secretary. She was seated behind a long counter doing some paperwork. Miss Brooks had worked at Taylor Elementary for many years. People called her an old maid. And I had to admit she was pretty plain; about as plain as vanilla ice-cream. But I liked vanilla ice-cream and I liked her. She was always friendly.

"Hi, Miss Brooks," Brains said. "I heard there was another malicious act of vandalism on Friday night. I was wondering if the police have any idea as to who the perpetrator might be."

I had to admit. Brains knew how to talk to grownups.

"Unfortunately no," she said. "Mr. Padget (he was our school's principal) believes it's a student. But I honestly don't know. What child attending here who would do such a thing? All the students are so good!"

See what I mean? There were a lot of kids I didn't trust as far as I could throw them and I could think of four or five guys off the top of my head who would *do such a thing*. But Miss Brooks thought the best of everyone. She just couldn't believe that a student here would misbehave so.

We thanked Miss Brooks and left.

"Well she obviously wouldn't do it," I said once we were in the hallway.

"Nonetheless, Operative Three, we need to check everyone, I believe our suspect has a key to the school."

We walked down the hallway looking classrooms. Most of the doors were still closed and I imagined that the teachers were in the teachers' lounge.

"Well we just batted a big fat zero," I said after we had walked up and down the first and second floors of the school.

This private detective work was harder than I thought!

I guess we will have to reconnoiter during lunch," Brains said.

"Huh?"

"Reconnoiter. To meet and gather information."

"Ohhh!"

Now I knew Brains definitely read a dictionary for kicks!

"We must verify that the lunch ladies are innocent," Brains said.

"Oh, yeah," I said. "Crime in a hairnet. And I'm not just talking about our lunches!"

I laughed. I thought I was being pretty witty, but Brains ignored my comment and said that he would keep walking up and down the hallways observing the teachers until the bell rang.

I meanwhile went to my post and made sure nobody ran.

Jimmy Carson, Safety Patrol!

The morning seemed to crawl along like a snail in a retirement home. I was chomping at the bit for lunch and X's report. You see, even though Brains and I are in different classes, we still have the same lunch period.

We met up near the front of the cafeteria and went through the lunch line together.

"Any luck?" I asked.

"None, Operative Three. None at all."

We checked out everybody we saw who was working behind the glass counters. Nothing! We had seen just about everyone except maybe one person who was way in the back doing dishes.

"Man! I thought that this would be easier, X!"

"*Adopt the pace of nature,* Operative Three. *Her secret is patience.*"

Patience? I wasn't good at patience!

"What clown said that?" I asked between mouthfuls of Jell-O, hamburger, and tater tots.

Brains looked at me as if I had two heads.

"I don't believe he ever labored under the big top," he replied dryly, "but it was Ralph Waldo Emerson."

"Oh!" I replied.

I guess Brains read more than the dictionary!

I sat in my class daydreaming. Which of course meant my teacher would call on me."

"Jimmy?"

"Ah, yes, ma'am?"

"Care to answer the question?"

"Umm, what was it again?"

This caused everyone in class to burst out laughing.

I felt my cheeks burn red.

"Who said, '*Do not go where the path may lead, go instead where there is no path and leave a trail.*'"

I was stumped. But I took a shot in the dark. "Um, Ralph Waldo Emerson?"

Mrs. Winter looked stunned. Then she smiled and said, "Correct."

I looked around the room grinning. *Yeah, I answered it y'all!*

Even though my Safety Patrol spot was in just in front of the school, I still got to leave class fifteen minutes early.

I was shocked to see Chief Hadley and Officer McKeon standing in the hallway in front of the main office. They were talking to Mr. Padget and Mrs. Robinson, the kitchen manager.

When they saw me coming they went into the main office. But not before I heard them talking.

Apparently someone had stolen over one hundred dollars from the school cafeteria!

The Vandal

Chapter 5

I went out to the sidewalk in front of the main entrance and paced back and forth like a hungry wolf.

I couldn't believe it! Taylor Elementary School was in the midst of a crime wave!

I couldn't wait to tell Brains!

The bell finally rang and students spilled out of their classrooms. They stampeded like a herd cattle through the hallways. They hit the nearest exit with the roar of shouts and laughter.

I watched the first wave of kids flow out the front doors totally ignoring my duty to make sure the kids didn't run.

At last I saw a flash of red hair. I frantically waved for Brains to come over.

"Did you spot the perpetrator, Operative Three," he asked excitedly.

"No, X, but money was stolen from the school cafeteria!"

I hadn't known Brains long, but I realized later this was one of the rare times that I would ever see him surprised.

"Chief Hadley and Officer McKeon are in the office talking to Mr. Padget and Mrs. Robinson," I continued.

"Excellent!" Brains gushed excitedly. "With Mrs. Robinson in the office, it gives us a chance to go investigate the scene of the crime. Quickly, Operative Three. The game is afoot!"

"What?" I said. "The game is a foot?"

I looked down at my sneakers then up at Brains.

He looked like he wanted to slug me.

"Just follow me!" he snapped.

We pushed our way upstream against the stragglers leaving the school and headed down the hallway to the cafeteria.

When we got there the chairs were all turned upside-down and placed top of the tables. Mr. Jefferies, the school janitor, was off in a corner mopping the floor.

We went toward the doors that the lunch lines went through but they were closed.

Brains turned a knob. It was locked.

"Can I help you boys?"

It was Mr. Jefferies. He had stopped mopping and was standing there watching us.

"No, sir," Brains said. "We were just looking for Mrs. Robinson."

"Well she's not back there boys."

"Okay, Thank you," Brains said.

Together we walked out the door.

"Did you see it?" Brains asked.

"See what?"

"Mr. Jefferies."

"Yeah, I saw Mr. Jefferies."

Again Brain looked like he wanted to slug me.

"Mr. Jefferies was wearing gloves on his hands," Brains said.

"Say! You're right!" I exclaimed. "He might have a bandage under there. Have you seen him today?"

"No."

"Neither have I!"

"We should stake out the faculty parking lot and see if he has a cut on his hand," Brains said.

We were standing outside the cafeteria when I said, "Oh, no. It's Stony Rhodes!"

"What's wrong with that?" Brains asked.

"He's the captain of patrols, and I left my post early!"

Stony came strutting up like a peacock in a spotlight.

"Carson, why aren't you at your post?" he asked while puffing his chest out.

The way he did it you couldn't help but notice his blue patrol belt compared to my dumb white one.

"I ah---"

"I asked Jimmy to assist me in looking for my wallet," Brains interrupted. "I believed I'd lost it in the cafeteria, and we just found it." Brains flashed his wallet as proof. "Your safety patrols are a credit to your leadership."

Stony just stood there with his mouth open.

Suddenly, the bell rang.

"Opps! Guess I'm off duty," I said. "See you tomorrow, Stony. And close your mouth. It's not dignified!"

Brains and I walked off leaving Stony Rhodes one confused fella.

"Operative Three, let's go by the custodial room."

"Why?" I asked.

"We have two crimes. One is vandalism, the second is a robbery. I don't believe that it's a coincidence but rather one person responsible for both."

"Mr. Jefferies? But why?"

"I don't know. But if he stole the money it might be in his room."

Creeps! This was getting worse and worse!

We walked down to a small side hallway. The custodial room was in the corner and the door was closed.

"I'll stay here and keep watch, Operative Three. You go try the door."

"Gotch-ya, X!"

I walked down the small alcove.

Turning a doorknob is such an easy thing. But as I reached out for it, my hand felt as heavy as lead.

The butterflies in my stomach were doing barrel rolls and I could hear my heart pumping in my ears as I my fingers closed around the knob. I turned it.

Nothing, it didn't budge.

"It's locked, X!" I stage whispered.

Brains turned around and looked at me.

"Let's go out the door."

Brains walked down the small hallway to me and we pushed our way outside.

"What should we do?" I asked.

"I believe our next move should be to stakeout the custodial room from here. Hopefully we will learn something."

Brains and I were in a small courtyard. A sidewalk led to the parking lot. We took a seat on a bench and waited.

We didn't have to wait long, though. Mr. Jefferies went into his room.

"What now?" I asked.

"I believe he is going to come out this way. We will then have an opportunity to confront him."

Confront him? Had Brains lost his marbles? Mr. Jefferies might be an old guy, but he was easily stronger than the two of us.

I was about to ask Brains what he meant when suddenly Mr. Jefferies came back out of his room.

Sure enough, just as Brains had said he came out the side door and started walking right towards us!

Brains stood up. But all I could do was sit on the bench like a bump on a log.

"Good afternoon, Mr. Jefferies," Brains said in a pleasant voice.

"Oh, hi," Mr. Jefferies responded. You could tell by his tone he was surprised to see anybody.

"That looks like a nasty cut on your hand," Brains said.

I looked. The gloves were off and you could see that blood had oozed through some taped gauze.

"Aw, it's nothing. You tend to get a bit banged up in his line of work."

He started to walk away. As he did I noticed he made a small jingly sound like he was walking with spurs.

Brains followed and I got up.

"Mr. Jefferies," Brains said. "The school has been vandalized for three weeks running."

"Yeah, I know, I've had to clean up the glass. In fact that's how I cut myself."

"The vandal cut himself too," Brains said. "He did it by punching a rock through the window and pushing it too far."

Mr. Jefferies stopped and turned around.

"Really" he said.

"Not only that," Brains continued, "but I believe the same person also stole money from the cafeteria today. And they stole a lot of coins which would make a sound like you are making."

Mr. Jefferies stared at Brains. Then his eyes went wide as saucers..

He turned and started to run.

"After him!" Brains yelled.

Mr. Jefferies might have been stronger than we were, but he wasn't faster. I caught up to him in no time flat.

I jumped on his back. But if I was expecting him to go down I was sadly mistaken. He just kept running like I was a back pack or something.

The next thing I knew, we started to go down. Brains and tackled Jefferies and taken his legs out from under him.

We both crash landed with a thud. Money spilled out like confetti onto the grass.

I didn't know what to expect next, but it sure wasn't what happened next.

I climbed off Jefferies. I half expected him to get up and start running again. But he didn't. He just sat there on his knees and put his head in his hands.

When he finally lifted his head I could see tears in his eyes.

"I had kids like you," Mr. Jefferies said. "They're all grown now." He stopped. "I taught them right from wrong. But I…"

His voice drifted off like fog.

"Boys, I was told last month that the school was forcing me to retire at the end of the school year in a few weeks. I was planning to work another five years. Heck, I need to work five more years!" He shook his head. "I was so mad I decided to make them pay. If they weren't going to pay me they could pay for the broken windows! And then today when I went into Mrs. Robinson's office and saw all the money, I couldn't help myself."

Brains and I stood there looking at him.

"I guess I had better turn myself in," he said.

I wasn't so sure I trusted him, but we helped him gather all the money up and he jammed it back into his pants pocket.

"I don't know how you did it, boys. How you discovered it was me. But I thank you. I hated what I was doing. And today I made things worse. I have to go take my come-uppins. It's what I taught my kids."

Mr. Jefferies stood up, nodded at us and said, "You're good boys. Stay that way."

"Yes, sir," Brains and I chorused

He turned and headed back inside.

Brains and I followed him at a distance. We watched as he turned and slowly walked up the main hallway.

I sort of felt bad for the guy.

As he neared the main office, Chief Hadley, Officer McKeon, Mr. Padget, and Mrs. Robinson all came out.

Mr. Jefferies walked straight up to them.

As he talked, they all looked shocked, like a kid who had just stuck a barrette into a wall outlet.

After a bit Jefferies looked back and saw us. He pointed at Brains and me and said something.

Chief Hadley didn't look happy, but Officer McKeon smiled and tipped his cap at us. Mr. Padget just scratched his head while Mrs. Robinson looked like she couldn't understand what Jefferies was saying.

"Come on, Jimmy, let's go."

Brains and I turned and walked out the back of the school.

A few days later I found myself once again out behind the Benton's garage. I had pushed my way through the bushes and pressed the nail. A metallic voice said, "State your name."

"Jimmy," I said.

Nothing happened.

"State your name," the voice said again.

"Oh, ah, Jimmy Carson!"

Still nothing.

I was beginning to think something was wrong with the secret entrance way, so I tried to slide it open with the palm of my hands.

"State-your-name!"

Although the voice was low and metallic, I could tell it was ticked-off.

Then it hit me.

"Ohhh! Umm, Operative Three."

The panel slid open and I stepped inside.

I guess I still had to learn the ropes about in this private detective thing. But you know what? I was excited about learning it with Brains.

I liked the idea just fine!

Milton Keynes UK
Ingram Content Group UK Ltd.
UKHW030620140324
439439UK00002B/344